BILLIE THE WILD CHILD

Also by Hannah Shaw

**KITTEN LADY'S BIG BOOK
OF LITTLE KITTENS**

Adventures in Fosterland series

**EMMETT AND JEZ
SUPER SPINACH
BABY BADGER
SNOWPEA THE PUPPY QUEEN**

KITTEN LADY
HANNAH SHAW

Adventures in FOSTERLAND

Illustrated by
Bev Johnson

BILLIE THE WILD CHILD

This book is a work of fiction. Any references to historical events, real people, or real places are used fictitiously. Other names, characters, places, and events are products of the author's imagination, and any resemblance to actual events or places or persons, living or dead, is entirely coincidental.

ALADDIN

An imprint of Simon & Schuster Children's Publishing Division
1230 Avenue of the Americas, New York, New York 10020
First Aladdin paperback edition April 2024
Copyright © 2024 by Kitten Lady, LLC.
Also available in an Aladdin hardcover edition.
All rights reserved, including the right of reproduction in whole or in part in any form.
ALADDIN and related logo are registered trademarks of Simon & Schuster, LLC.
Simon & Schuster: Celebrating 100 Years of Publishing in 2024
For information about special discounts for bulk purchases, please contact
Simon & Schuster Special Sales at 1-866-506-1949 or business@simonandschuster.com.
The Simon & Schuster Speakers Bureau can bring authors to your live event. For
more information or to book an event contact the Simon & Schuster
Speakers Bureau at 1-866-248-3049 or visit our website at www.simonspeakers.com.
Designed by Tiara Iandiorio
The illustrations for this book were rendered digitally.
The text of this book was set in Banda.
Manufactured in the United States of America 0324 OFF
2 4 6 8 10 9 7 5 3 1
Library of Congress Cataloging-in-Publication Data
Names: Shaw, Hannah René, 1987- author. | Johnson, Bev, illustrator.
Title: Billie the wild child / by Hannah Shaw ; illustrated by Bev Johnson.
Description: First Aladdin paperback edition. | New York : Aladdin, 2024. |
Series: Adventures in Fosterland | Summary: When three ducklings arrive in Fosterland,
it is the white mallard, Billie, who feels different than the others, and though he likes
being in there with his friends he sometimes longs to be free in the wild.
Identifiers: LCCN 2023032962 (print) | LCCN 2023032963 (ebook) |
ISBN 9781665936408 (hc) | ISBN 9781665936392 (pbk) | ISBN 9781665936415 (ebook)
Subjects: CYAC: Foster care of animals—Fiction. | Ducks—Fiction. | Animals—
Infancy—Fiction. | Self perception—Fiction. | Friendship—Fiction. | BISAC: JUVENILE
FICTION / Readers / Chapter Books | JUVENILE FICTION / Family / Orphans &
Foster Homes | LCGFT: Animal fiction.
Classification: LCC PZ7.1.S4935 Bi 2024 (print) | LCC PZ7.1.S4935 (ebook) | DDC [Fic]—dc23
LC record available at https://lccn.loc.gov/2023032962
LC ebook record available at https://lccn.loc.gov/2023032963

To everyone who dreams of
spreading their wings

Contents

CHAPTER 1

I Am Not a Pet!

Thump. Thump. Thump.

Billie shuffled around in the darkness, his orange webbed feet sliding against cardboard. With every rise and fall, he bumped against the other ducklings . . . or were they bumping into him? He couldn't quite tell! All he knew was that he and his friends were stuffed into a box together and that they were being carried far away from the only home he knew.

Since hatching, Billie and his friends had lived at Sunny Lake. Every day, Billie would line up in a row with the other ducklings and waddle through the grass, one after another, hopping in the water for a nice, cool dip. Oh, how he loved that lake! Being one of eight duck- lings meant that he had plenty of pals to splash around with, and whenever it was time to go for a walk, he always knew exactly where to go as long as he stayed in line with the others.

But on this day something had gone wrong. He'd followed them straight into a drainage pipe, where all they could do was peep and cheep for help.

Now, thumping about in that box, Billie found himself confused and dis-gruntled. He was grateful that some-one had helped him and his friends out of the pipe, but stuffing them into a pitch-black box seemed more than a little uncalled for!

"That's humans for you," one of the ducklings said. "They can't be trusted."

Billie tried to peer through the little holes in the cardboard, but he couldn't see a thing. "Where are they taking us?" he asked. But no one knew.

Finally, with one last *thud*, the box landed on a hard, flat surface. The eight ducklings looked toward the sky, watching as the flaps of the box opened one by one. But as the light flooded in, Billie didn't see clouds or sunshine. He saw bright electric lighting overhead, partially covered by shadowy human faces looking down at him.

The ducklings erupted with startled peeps at the sight of the humans. "Nope, nope, nope," Billie grumbled as he wedged himself between his downy pals. "I'm *not* a people duck."

The people muttered and pointed with their long, wiggling fingers, and Billie tried to hide behind the others and close his eyes. But when he peeked through one suspicious eye, he could

have sworn the humans were all pointing directly at *him*.

Being part of a group meant he had
never been singled out in his life. "Why
me?" Billie asked, trying again to blend
into the crowd. But now the giant fingers

were getting closer and closer, writhing in pursuit of Billie and Billie alone.

A cold hand wrapped around his little lemon-colored body and pulled him away from the others as he repeated, "Why me?!"

He wriggled and writhed and nibbled fingers with his tiny beak, doing everything he could to express himself as he was carried away from the wildlife center and toward a door marked SMALL PETS. The human plopped Billie into a bin on a shelf, along with a stuffed animal in the shape of a baby chick and some tiny bowls containing water and dry pellets. But none of this appealed to him—he needed to know where he was and, more important, how to get to the exit!

"Where is my flock? What is this horrible holding cell you've placed me in?" He flipped over the bowl of pellets to signal his disapproval. "I don't belong here!"

A small voice snickered in the cage to his right. It was a small, furry animal who looked similar to the muskrats who used to swim around the lake.

"Mr. Muskrat! Can you help me? Can you tell me how to get back to the lake?" Billie begged.

"*Muskrat?*" the animal replied. "Young sir, I am no muskrat. I am a guinea pig. And I know nothing about any lake. Besides, the only water I need is right here," he said, sticking out his tongue and licking a metal ball at the end of a water bottle. "Also, my name is Tofu Taco the Third."

Billie tilted his head in confusion. He had never met a guinea pig before and had never heard such a silly name in all his life.

While Tofu focused on his water bottle, Billie tried another neighbor. He turned to his left and was relieved to see what he thought was a wild hare. "Oh, Ms. Rabbit! You should be out hopping around in the grass! But you're here, stuck in a cage . . . Don't you miss the outside? Haven't you tried to escape?"

"Outside?" laughed the rabbit,

who introduced herself as Cupcake Sprinkles. "Can't say I've ever been. My last home was a condo."

Billie's head was spinning. Who were these animals with funny names who knew nothing of the wonders of nature? "But . . . animals belong out-side," Billie said. "Don't they?"

"Let me explain something," Tofu Taco III began, clearing his throat. "There are two types of animals: wild animals and domestical . . . domestic . . . domesticalated."

". . . Domesticated," Cupcake Sprinkles chimed in, nodding.

"Yeah, what she said. Anyway, wild animals go to the wildlife center down the hall, and once they're healthy, they go back and live in nature where they belong. You know, field mice, baby raccoons, songbirds . . . Animals like that. But not us. We're pets, so we stay here in the adoption center. That is, until a human gives us a forever home."

Billie tensed up. "I am not a pet!" he insisted.

"But of course you are," laughed Tofu Taco III, who was starting to get on his nerves. "Just look at you."

"I'm a *duck*!" Billie shouted. "Hello, can't you see my little wings? My tail feathers?" He shook his tail to make his point.

Tofu Taco III smirked. "Well, there

are wild ducks and there are pet ducks. You are here in the 'Small Pets' room, so . . . you are clearly a pet."

"And clearly small!" Cupcake Sprinkles giggled.

Billie fell to the floor and sighed heavily through his little orange beak.

"Don't be sad! Being a pet is great," Cupcake Sprinkles explained. "From here, you'll either go to a foster home or an adopter. You just have to wait for a person to come here and fall in love with you."

"Fall in what?! I don't think so. I'm a *wild* duck! I'm not trying to fall in love with any humans. Trust me, there's been some kind of huge mistake here.

Just watch: any minute now, they'll be here to bring me back to the wildlife center, and then my flock and I will be on our way back to Sunny Lake."

Soon enough, a person arrived and picked up Billie in his bin. He looked to the small animals and stuck out his tongue as if to say *I told you so.* He wouldn't have to stay in the adoption center and be given a silly name like Peanut Butter Sandwich or Ice Cream Cone, or worse! Now—he hoped—he could return to a dignified life on the water. "Smell ya later!" he shouted as he waved goodbye with his tiny wing.

But instead of heading toward the wildlife center, Billie watched from his bin as he passed through the streets. Stuck between four clear walls, all he could do was watch his fate unfold before him. Eventually, they stopped at the front door of a house. The door creaked open, and a human stood in the doorway, collecting him and bringing him inside.

A small white cat peeked out from behind the human's leg, softly saying, "Welcome to Fosterland."

CHAPTER 2

I Am Not Cute!

Billie awoke the next morning with tall plastic walls surrounding him on all sides. The human—who he now considered "the guard"—had placed him in some kind of large holding area, where he was being kept against his will.

Everything felt artificial. The air was stagnant, with not a hint of breeze. The ground was composed of smooth wood, with no grass or dirt or worms. The usual soundtrack of crickets and frogs was replaced by an eerie silence, the only sound being the hum of the small refrigerator across the room.

Billie huffed as he paced in a circle, grumbling to himself. "Pet duck. Well, I never! Just wait till the others hear about this. . . ."

Set on escaping, he thought about how the grown-up ducks at the lake would flap their wings and fly. He closed his eyes, took a deep breath, and tried to envision the wind beneath his wings, carrying him through the air. The thought alone made him feel calm and at ease.

He flapped his wings . . . and nothing happened.

Furrowing his brow, Billie stood up tall and tried again. But he remained on the floor.

Billie's wings looked like two tiny triangles thinly coated with yellow fuzz. And no matter how hard he flapped them, his little fluffy body stayed exactly where it was. "Rrrruh!" he called out as he leapt and flapped over and over, trying desperately to fly.

"Ah, pond scum!" Why wasn't it working?

He stomped to the other side of his pen, where breakfast had been laid out for him by the guard. While he wasn't keen on eating the strange prepared meal earlier, the truth was that all that flapping had now made him very, very hungry.

What is all this? Billie wondered as he sniffed the dishes. Usually, he would spend the whole day searching the lakeside for insects and larvae and bits of plants in the water, but here he seemed to have a full day's worth of food just sitting in a bowl.

First, he tried a bit of the porridge. "It's fine, I guess," he said aloud. Less fun than digging for worms, though.

Next, he tried a bite of the leafy greens. "That's actually pretty nice. Good texture, a bit of grassy flavor . . ."

And finally, it was time to sample a blueberry. He looked at the small round fruit, never having seen anything like it in his life. The blueberry was so big—or perhaps he was so small—that he could hardly place his beak around it. Slowly, he opened his mouth as wide as he could and bit down on the ripe fruit.

Pop! Berry juice spilled into his mouth.

It was the most delicious thing he'd ever tasted! He began gobbling berries as quickly as he could. *Pop, gulp, pop, gulp, pop!* Sweet blue liquid burst in his mouth and dribbled down his throat, coating his yellow baby feathers in sticky juice.

"Looks like you're enjoying your-
self!" came a voice from the doorway.
It was Eloise, the one-eyed white cat
who had welcomed him to Fosterland.
She sauntered toward him with her tail
swishing.

Billie was so shocked to see her that

he swallowed a berry whole with a loud *gulp!* He turned around and stood up as tall as he could, which was only about three inches high. "It's not what it looks like. I am *not* enjoying myself! Actually, I demand to know where I am and why I'm being held like some sort of prisoner. . . ."

Eloise smirked. "Whoa there, little guy. This is far from a prison. This is Fosterland! It's a wonderful place where any baby animal would be happy to grow up while they wait for their forever home. We proudly serve puppies and piglets and oh-so-many kittens and, of course, cute little ducklings like you."

Billie stomped his foot adorably. "I am *not cute*!"

Eloise smiled, seeming to wink. "Sure you aren't."

"Listen, this might be a great place for puppies and piglets and kittens, but it isn't the place for me," Billie explained. "I don't belong here. I'm supposed to be with the other ducklings."

Eloise knew just what to say. "Well, you're in for a real treat, then . . . because there are two other ducklings here waiting to be your friends."

"There are?" Billie perked up. He hadn't seen another duckling in a whole day!

"There are," Eloise replied. "They're

just in the other room with all the kittens, getting checked in for foster care. I'm sure they'll join you any minute now."

Billie sighed, relieved to hear that he would have other ducklings to talk to soon. Surely they would understand him. Maybe they could even help lead him back to the lake! He sat up tall and tried to groom some of the blueberry juice from his neck, hoping to make a good first impression.

CHAPTER 3

I Am Not Striped?

Down the hallway, the sound of singing was getting closer and closer.

"Blueberries and creeeaaam!" squawked a voice in a musical tone.

"Ain't it just a dreeeaaam!" a second voice belted out comically.

Billie looked to the doorway. The guard was approaching, and she was carrying a box with two singing ducklings inside. She placed the box into Billie's pen, then tilted it gently.

Billie watched with great anticipation as two larger ducklings tap-danced their way out of the box, singing over one another and laughing with delight.

These ducklings looked nothing like his friends at all. They were goofy, gigantic, and strangest of all, they were bright yellow. But none of that mattered—they were ducklings!

"Eep! Well, aren't you just adorable!" said one duckling to Billie, bending over to take a look at him.

"Oh my! That's the tiniest duckling I've ever seen!" said the other, poking him with her beak. "Is he real?"

"Yes, I'm real!" Billie peeped. "I'm Billie! And it is good to see you two! I've just had the strangest couple of days. First I was in a box . . . and then I was in another box . . . and then . . . there were rabbits and guinea pigs and a cat, and, well . . . no one could understand my predicament!"

"Billie, nice to meet you," said the duckling with the spotted beak. "I'm Marlie."

"And I'm Charlie! We're sisters. Can ya tell?" said the other duckling as she bumped tail feathers with Marlie. "So, tell us . . . what's the problem?"

Billie gestured toward the walls. "Well, isn't it obvious? All of us are stuck here, and we can't get out!" he cried. He looked around to make sure the guard and Eloise were gone, then leaned in and quietly said, "But don't worry. I'm already plotting our escape." Or at least he was plotting to plot their escape. He didn't see any weaknesses in their holding cell now, but there had to be one somewhere.

"Escape?" Marlie screamed. "But we just got here!"

"Yeah, and the amenities are fantastic! Did you try the blueberries yet? They're heavenly!" Charlie added. Her feet started to dance yet again, and she momentarily broke back into song. "Blueberries and cream!"

Billie was confused. "Yeah, I tried them, and they're really good. But . . . don't you want to get out of here?"

The sisters shook their heads rapidly, their big orange beaks moving left to right over and over like flags in the wind. It was clear that they had no intention of leaving.

"You're . . . happy to be here?" Billie asked.

The sisters sang in unison: "Yesssss!"

Billie looked up at Marlie and Charlie, who were about four times his size. How was it possible they were interpreting this situation so positively? Why did he feel miserable, but they felt like singing and dancing? And . . . why did

they look so different from the ducklings at the pond?

"I don't mean to pry, but . . . where
are your stripes and spots?" he asked.

"Stripes and spots? Only wild ducklings look like that!" Marlie laughed.
"We're not wild ducks. We're pets."

"Yeah! That's why we're solid yellow,
just like you," Charlie agreed.

Billie's heart sank. What did they
mean by "just like" him?

Marlie continued. "You're thinking
of . . . what are they called, mallards?
Those are the wild ones with the brown
stripes and whatnot, right, Charlie?"

"Yeah, mallards! We learned about
them in school, remember?" Charlie

confirmed. "But we aren't mallards, you silly goose—er—duck! Ha ha! We're Pekins. That's why we're yellow, all three of us!"

Billie slowly turned his head to the side and tilted it dramatically, trying to get a look at his back. All of his friends at the lake had beautiful brown stripes and spots, and he always assumed he looked the same. But to his surprise, it appeared that Marlie and Charlie were right—he didn't have stripes after all.

"I'm . . . solid yellow?" Billie asked, confused.

"Bright as the sun!" Charlie replied. "And cute as a button."

Now Billie was really lost. All his

life he'd assumed he belonged in the wild, but if it was true that he looked just like Marlie and Charlie, then that explained why he had been separated from the others.

"Don't be so sad, little guy!" Marlie said, taking Billie under her tiny wing. "Fosterland is like paradise, can't you see? This is the best possible place for a duckling to end up. This is the good life."

"Yep. You are one lucky duck," Charlie agreed. "And don't forget, Fosterland is just a waystation. Someday, when we go to Foreverland, it'll be even better!"

Billie sat between them, thinking. His brain was swirling, but his body was comforted by the protective feeling of

their warmth and their feathers against his. At least he had some nice company while he sorted this all out. He burrowed down between them.

"You know, I'm happy we're here with you," Marlie said. "Where we came from, the future can be pretty uncertain. But now that we're here, things are looking up."

"Where did you come from?" Billie asked, tilting his head to gaze up at his new friend.

"Well, we were hatched in a classroom," Marlie explained. "It's fun for a while, but the truth of the matter is that so many of us end up abandoned . . . or brought to some awful farm. . . ."

"For two whole weeks you're passed around, held, and loved, and then— just like that—you're old news." Charlie looked down at her webbed feet. "And no one thinks about what happens to us after we go."

Billie had never heard of something

so horrible. "So that's how you ended up here?"

Marlie and Charlie nodded, and he could understand why they loved it as much as they did.

"We got really lucky. This is our chance at a happy future," Marlie said. "A future where we are really loved—forever."

"And the future looks even brighter now that the three of us are together!" Charlie added.

The ducklings sat in a silent huddle, smiling with their eyes shut. *An even brighter future*, Billie pondered to himself. He couldn't imagine a life better than the one he'd had at the lake, but if his new friends were right, he wondered if maybe he should give it a chance after all.

"A-one-two-three-four—" Marlie began to sing, tapping her foot. "Birds of a feather . . . We stick together . . ."

"Birds of a feather . . . Best friends forever!" Charlie sang along. "Everybody now!"

"Birds of a feather . . . We stick together . . . ," the two repeated, signaling for Billie to join them.

Billie lifted his tiny head toward them and sang, "Birds of a feather . . . Best friends forever?"

CHAPTER 4

Pool Party

The next morning was brighter indeed.

Billie, Marlie, and Charlie were carried to the back of the house, where a grassy backyard could be seen through a large sliding glass door. Billie's eyes widened at the sight of the blue sky over the green lawn, and as the door slid open, he squealed.

"Freedom!" Billie cheered as he speed-waddled into the yard.

The sunshine glistened on his fluff as a gentle breeze blew through it, and he peeped to the clouds above: "I'm free! Hello, sun! Hello, bugs! Hello, Earth! I'm free!"

More hesitant than their friend, Marlie and Charlie waddled after Billie, chirping and cheeping as they instinctively lined up in a row behind him. Billie, who was barely a quarter of their height, felt proud to be the leader of the pack.

"Follow me!" Billie chirped as the trio marched around the yard.

"The carpet is making me ticklish," Charlie giggled.

"That's grass—is this really your first time walking on it?" Billie asked, surprised.

Charlie nodded and laughed. "It's fun!"

Billie headed toward a bright blue ramp that led to the top of a large circular tub. He curiously stepped up, and as he reached the top, he looked down and couldn't believe his eyes.

It was full of water!

"It's . . . a fake lake!" he screamed, and hopped inside the pool without a second thought.

Marlie and Charlie stood side by side at the top of the ramp, looking down at Billie as he paddled around. "What are you waiting for?" he asked. "Dive in— the water is perfect!"

"Here goes nothing!" Marlie said as she and Charlie leapt into the pool. *Splash!* Little water droplets sprayed Billie's face as the duo joined him, and he couldn't stop smiling.

"Whoa! This is awesome!" Charlie remarked. "I've never been in the water before!"

"Look at us go!" Marlie giggled, paddling hard. "We're doing it!"

Billie's tiny orange flipper-feet moved speedily under the water. "Bet you can't catch me!" he said, darting around the pool.

Marlie flapped her baby wings as hard as she could, splashing water all around and cracking up. "This is the *best*!"

"Look, I'm a water fountain," Charlie joked as she spit water out over her head.

"Check this out," Billie said, eager to impress his friends. He stretched up, took a deep breath, and dove deep under the water, swimming far underneath them. Billie could hold his breath for an impressive amount of time, and he zoomed below their feet as they stared from above with mouths agape.

"How does he do that?" Marlie shrieked. "He's like a fish!"

Pop! After some time, Billie's tiny yellow head popped back out of the water, and he shook the water droplets from his head, grinning. "Ta-da! I call it 'deep-sea diving.' One of my favorite activities."

Marlie and Charlie stared, amazed. For a tiny guy, Billie sure seemed to know a lot about swimming.

"This is the best pool party I've ever been to," Charlie said.

"It's the *only* pool party you've ever been to, you goofball," Marlie replied.

"Yeah . . . and it's the best!" Charlie cheered. "The only thing that could possibly make this better would be poolside snacks. Does Fosterland offer an outdoor menu, or . . . ?"

Billie knew just what to do. "You know, the tastiest snacks are all around us already. Have you ever tried . . . a sky raisin?"

"What's a sky raisin?" the girls asked in cheery unison.

"They're these little black snacks that fly around in the air and sound like this: *buzzzzz*. Listen carefully, and you'll hear as they get closer."

The three sat silently, listening and watching. Suddenly, a fly started to zip by them.

Billie whispered, "Now it's only a matter of waiting very patiently . . . until . . ." He stretched his neck toward the sky, snapped his beak, and nibbled proudly. "And that's how you catch a sky raisin!"

"That seems pretty complicated . . . ,"
Marlie said.

"A lot harder than just eating out of a dish," Charlie added. "Isn't there some organic lettuce or something we can have instead?"

"This is as organic as it gets!" Billie laughed. "Locally sourced, straight from the sky. Just try it!"

Snap! Snap! Snap! The two tried snapping their beaks at the passing flies, leaping over one another and causing a big splash. "Why do I feel like I'm not graceful enough for this?" Charlie giggled, shaking the water from her face.

Snap! Marlie caught her first sky raisin. "Look at me! I did it!" Crunching, she said, "And, hey . . . that's pretty good!"

Charlie tried again. *Snap!* "I got one, too! Woo! You've got to admit it's no blueberries and cream . . . but it's still tasty!"

The trio spent the next hour splashing, laughing, and making a game out of who could catch the most sky raisins. And for the first time since getting pulled from the drain pipe, Billie didn't have a care in the world. It was just him and his friends having a perfect day.

Eventually, tired from swimming laps, the trio stepped back into the grass to dry off in the sun. As they preened their feathers, Billie stretched out his tiny wings and tried flapping them to fly.

"I can't get these darn things to work," he admitted, looking frustratingly at his side. "Do yours work?" he asked the others.

Charlie looked at him with a funny

face. "Don't be silly! Everyone knows pet ducks can't fly."

Billie gulped.

The more he learned about pet ducks, the more he was starting to question his identity. Deep down he *felt* like a wild duck, but now he wasn't sure what to think! His head and his heart were playing tug-of-war, and it was creating a great big lump in his throat. All he could do was swallow it down.

"Oh," he replied sadly. "Well, that explains that."

The sun was setting, and the guard came out to collect the ducks and bring them inside.

Marlie and Charlie willingly jumped

into the guard's arms, but Billie peeped grumpily and refused to join them.

"Come on, Billie. It's dinner time," Marlie said. "That was a fun day, but it's time to go inside."

"No," he said. He didn't want to go.

"Billie, humans are our friends. This is the person who feeds us blueberries!" Charlie insisted. "Don't you want to have some blueberries?"

Billie shook his head and began to waddle away, shouting, "Blueberries are just a tool they use to keep you from asking questions!"

The guard sat Marlie and Charlie by the door and began to walk toward the tiny defiant duckling.

"Nope!" Billie called out as he picked up speed. As the guard got closer, Billie ran in circles around the pool, sticking out his tongue and darting away from his pursuer. Each time she got close, he zipped out of her grip.

He cackled. "You can't catch me! I cannot be contained!"

Billie ran to the edge of the yard, where he was stopped by a tall wooden barrier. He looked side to side, suddenly realizing that he was not as free as he thought: the entire yard was surrounded by a tall wooden fence. There was no escaping her approach; he was contained after all.

"It's okay Billie," Marlie said as they

hopped into their indoor enclosure together, where dinner awaited their return. "Don't be sad. I'm sure we'll get to go outside again tomorrow."

CHAPTER 5

Duck, Duck, Cat

Over the next week, Billie came to understand that pool time was, in fact, part of his new daily routine. In the morning, the guard would give him and his friends their breakfast of berries and mash, and then they'd go out to the backyard. Marlie and Charlie would do cannonballs into the water, Billie would practice his deep-sea diving moves, and then they'd sun themselves dry in the summer heat.

Every day, Billie would flap his wings and try to fly. He'd stand on the edge of the pool and jump off it, flapping wildly, before tumbling to the ground.

"I swear I got a little more lift that time!" Billie said one day as Marlie and Charlie floated lazily around the pool. "Did you see it?"

Marlie and Charlie just shook their heads and giggled. "Oh, Billie, you quack me up—pretending you can fly!" Charlie replied.

Billie grinned and shrugged. Deep down, nothing made him want to do something more than being told he couldn't do it! Even if he *was* a Pekin duck, he kept trying to fly anyway, hoping that maybe one day he would surprise them all.

Slowly, Billie was learning to enjoy his stay in Fosterland. Now that he and his friends were growing a little bigger, their enclosure walls had been removed, giving them full access to the nursery. And things had gotten way more interesting because they'd been joined by five fluffy kittens!

Billie had more in common with the kittens than he expected. First: they loved to run after one another just like little ducks in a row. Second: they had a variety of fun toys to nibble and play with. And third: they loved to cuddle in a pile when it was time to rest. They introduced Billie to comforts he'd never known, like soft blankets and plush beds. They even invited him to use their hideaway hut, which was shaped like a giant pineapple.

"Let's play a game!" suggested the little white kitten, Callooh, one day after the ducks had come in from their time outside.

"How about duck, duck, goose?" offered the gray-and-white kitten, Wabe.

"More like duck, duck, *cat*!" laughed Brillig, the gray one.

The eight friends sat in a circle and

took turns chasing after one another. And even though Billie's legs were substantially shorter than the others', he was the fastest of them all!

"Ha ha! You can't catch me!" he hollered gleefully as he was chased around the circle by Callay, the white kitten with black patches.

"So small but so nimble," Marlie noted.

"He's really something else," Charlie agreed.

After many rounds of duck, duck, cat, Billie was the clear winner, and everyone but him was totally exhausted. As they settled down, the guard came into the room and lay on the floor. All the worn-out kittens scampered over to where she lay and hopped on top of her as if she were some kind of cat bed herself. Their purrs echoed through the room as they lay with the human. For a moment, the three ducklings watched with their heads tilted. Then, Marlie and Charlie slowly waddled over and hopped into her lap, too, joining the five fluffy felines in a great big pile on the human's legs.

Billie had no interest in cuddling a human being. "I'll be in the pineapple if you guys need me."

One after another, the guard offered pets to each of the babies in her lap, who were getting sleepier by the min-

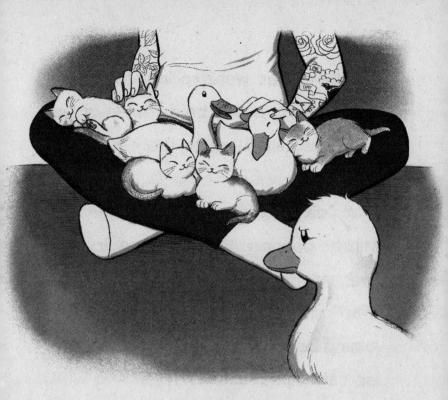

ute. When it was time for Marlie and Charlie to receive their back scratches, they leaned into the rubs, and their eyes rolled to the back of their heads in a state of absolute bliss. "This is the life," Marlie whispered, slowly falling asleep.

Billie's eyes were rolling, too. "You ducks might as well be a couple of lap cats!" he called out to them from his hidey hut.

A silky, blue-eyed calico named Mimsy opened her eyes and looked over at him. "What's so bad about that?" she asked. "You might consider joining us some day, you know. Being a lap cat has its . . . purrrrrks." And with that, she and the others closed their eyes and melted into the lap pile, leaving Billie to sit in the hut alone.

CHAPTER 6

The Other Side of the Window

Pitter-patter, pitter-patter. Billie awoke to the sound of rain against the roof of the nursery. He was squished in the middle of his seven friends, who had eventually come to join him in bed and whose feathers and fur surrounded him in a cozy blanket of love. He had to admit: it felt good to be snuggled.

"Sorry, guys—no outside time today,"

Eloise said as she walked into the nursery and hopped into a window bed to look out at the downpour. The dark clouds promised it would be gloomy and gray all day. "It's really coming down out there."

"It's raining cats and ducks!" Brillig joked, and Marlie and Charlie both snort-laughed.

Because they couldn't have outside time, the ducklings would have to spend the whole day doing indoor kitten activities.

"So what exactly do you guys do all day?" Billie asked.

"Well, it depends," Callooh explained. "Today is arts and crafts day!"

"We're going to make hats!" Callay declared, pawing through a pile of colorful paper. "Paper hats of every variety."

"I'm going to make a fedora," said Wabe. "Brillig, you need a top hat!"

Mimsy was already hard at work on a tea hat with a big purple bow. "Mine's going to be fancy . . . just like me," she said.

Marlie and Charlie had never worn a hat, but they were interested to try them, and they settled on matching party hats with pom-poms on top. "What about you, Billie?"

Billie looked at the craft supplies, and his heart began to race. Something about doing arts and crafts just didn't feel like *him*. "I'm good," he said.

But the kittens insisted that he join the fun. "I know just what you need!" Callay said cheerily, and made him a tiny headband with cat ears.

"Now you're one of us!" Brillig joked as they put the cat ears on Billie's fluffy yellow head.

But Billie didn't feel like one of them. In fact, the cat ears felt less like a fun game and more like a bad joke. Why was he inside making arts and crafts with little spoiled kittens when he could be outside splashing around in puddles? He looked around at the others and suddenly felt an incredible urge to go away.

He took a deep breath and shook the

cat ears from his head. "I'm sorry, guys, but this isn't for me," he said, and hopped into the windowsill next to Eloise.

As the kittens and ducklings played in their silly hats, Billie sat looking longingly out the window. Outside, the pavement was glittering with raindrops, and the lawn was moist with puddles. Unlike the others, he didn't mind that kind of weather one bit. He knew that just like the sunshine brings happiness—in the form of warmth and sky raisins—rain brings happiness in other ways.

He imagined all the little worms coming out from their hiding places and the squishy feeling of wet dirt under his webbed feet. He pictured himself splashing through the puddles in search of tasty grubs. He sighed heavily

"M'lady," Wabe said as he tipped his fedora to Mimsy, and they both laughed. But Billie paid no attention to their make-believe. He was fixated on the window, gazing past his reflection, pondering the thin, clear barrier that separated him from the natural world.

Suddenly, a flash of fur darted across the lawn. Billie watched with eyes wide as a fluffy feline stopped to drink fresh rainwater that had collected in a crack in the sidewalk. "Is that . . . a cat?" He looked to Eloise, stunned. "Outside?!"

"That's so sad," Callooh interjected, skipping around the others in a circle. "Cats shouldn't be out there in the rain. They belong inside, warm and toasty . . ."

". . . and with a variety of paper hats!" said Brillig, tilting his top hat.

"I pity that ol' tom," Callay said. "It must be sad to be a lost cat."

Billie looked out at the cat in the rain, then looked to Eloise for answers.

"He isn't lost," Eloise told them. "That's just Rufus, the neighborhood tomcat. He lives outside."

"I'll never understand that," sighed Mimsy as she gingerly licked her paw, fancy tea hat atop her fluffy head.

Eloise explained, "Well, it's simple. Some cats don't want to live inside, and Rufus is one of them. Cozy is comfortable, but, you know . . . feral is free."

Free. Billie's heart swelled at the word.

Thunder cracked, and the kittens and ducklings jumped and scattered. But Billie and Eloise stayed seated in the window, taking in the sounds of the storm outside. Billie watched as the mysterious cat's fluffy tail disappeared around the corner. Rufus was gone from sight but not from Billie's mind.

"Can I ask you a question?" he finally said. "Why is it that we live on this side

of the glass and Rufus lives on the other side?"

Eloise looked at Billie. Even with all the wonders that Fosterland had to offer, it seemed that he was torn about where he really belonged.

She laid a paw on his head and softly spoke in verse:

"Some kittens are
born to be lap cats,
And others are
born to be wild.
The journey toward
a place called home
Is a path that
begins as a child.

**Some cats are
in-betweeners
And feel home on
either side.
But only the cat knows
where he belongs—
And only the
cat decides."**

Billie sniffed and blinked away a tear that welled up. If a cat could decide where he belongs, then a duck should be able to, too.

He took a deep breath, nodded at Eloise, and knew exactly what he wanted to do.

CHAPTER 7

Splish-Splash, Mad Dash

That night, to make up for their canceled pool time, the guard drew a bath where the three ducklings could swim indoors. Testing the water with her fingers, she swirled it with her hand, turned off the faucet, then placed the ducks on the edge of the bathtub to show them their swimming quarters for the evening.

"An indoor pool!" Marlie cheered, diving in. "This is livin' in luxury, bay-bay!"

Charlie dove in and did a backstroke. "Oh yeah! A little slice of heaven!"

But Billie stood on the side, his webbed feet planted firmly against the ceramic edge of the tub. He looked at the water, which was pristine and clear and in a big white basin. It just didn't feel natural. He cleared his throat and took a deep breath.

"I'm leaving soon," Billie said matter-of-factly, his voice echoing against the tile walls. "I've decided that I don't belong here."

"What?" Charlie shrieked. "Of course

you belong! We're birds of a feather—best friends forever."

"That's very kind, and I would love to stay together. But not here. Not like this. I can't wear cat ears and swim in bathtubs. I belong out there, in the wild." He sniffled. "Come with me?"

Marlie and Charlie paused, their feet gently paddling in place, and stared at him. "We can't just choose to be wild, Billie," Marlie said. "First of all, it's dangerous out there. There's thunder and cars and probably monsters or something, too."

"Secondly," Charlie added, "there is no fruit out there! A life without fruit is no life at all."

"Thirdly . . . none of us can fly," Marlie said. Her words hit Billie like a dagger.

"You don't know that," Billie said with a lump in his throat. "I've been trying. Have you ever tried?"

"Maybe . . . Maybe we don't want to try!" Marlie said sharply. "Why won't you just accept the good life you've been given? Do you know how many hatchling birds sitting in kindergarten classrooms would long for the chance to come here and . . . float around in a claw-foot tub like some kind of . . . highfalutin rubber ducky?! Show some gratitude!"

"Just get in the bathtub, Billie," Charlie agreed. "Let's just forget the whole idea and have a nice night together. Besides, even if you wanted to escape, there is no way for you to break loose, anyway. You don't even have a plan!"

Billie sighed heavily and slipped into the tub, silently paddling in a circle and contemplating his situation. Although he felt frustrated that his friends couldn't understand him, he had to stay true to himself.

And he also knew something they didn't know: that he did have a plan after all.

That night, he fell asleep in the pine-apple hut with Marlie, Charlie, and the kittens, as always. But in the wee hours of the morning, when the first peek of the sun was coming through the windows and all of the house was silent and still, Billie tiptoed over his friends and quietly waddled to the front door.

Standing at the door, he looked around to make sure the guard wasn't around. For what felt like forever, he sat staring at the door, waiting patiently for the approaching footsteps of the mailman.

The mail slot finally clicked open. Billie leapt up, a tiny sliver of daylight peeking through the door as letters dropped to his feet. Swiftly, and without hesitation, he slipped through the

opening in the mail slot . . . and tumbled to the other side of the door, landing on a welcome mat.

Thud! His feathered butt hit the doormat, and he hopped to his feet.

He was free!

He shot a look to the mailman, who was walking away from the house, whistling without a care. *Ha! The mailman puts things* in *the slot—I suppose he doesn't expect for something to come* out, Billie snickered to himself with pride. He'd escaped, and no one had even noticed.

Looking out at the front yard, he could see that there was no fence at all to stop him from running away forever. As the sun peeked over the hillside, a colorful rainbow curved across the sky. The rain clouds were gone, and so were the walls and windows that had held him back for weeks and weeks.

Billie took a deep breath of fresh morning air and placed one foot on the dewy lawn. He'd made his choice . . . and there was no turning back now!

CHAPTER 8

A Walk in the Park

Squish-squish-squish! Billie waddled quickly through the front yard. "I did it! I really did it!" he cackled, quickly looking back to make sure that the guard wasn't watching from the window. As he made it to the sidewalk, he took a giant leap into a puddle, which splashed all around him. He was officially off the property of Fosterland!

With a great big belly laugh, he flapped his wings, which were growing stronger by the day.

"Where to?" he said to no one as he waddled down the road. "Wherever we want!" he answered himself, taking great delight in his newfound freedom.

He followed a floral fragrance into a vibrant garden down the road, which was bursting with colorful flowers and lush greenery. Shoving his beak into the petals of a rose, he inhaled deeply and let out a satisfied "aah." The scent of nature surrounded him, and it smelled sweet!

Bzz! A flying bug buzzed past, but just before he snapped his beak at it,

Billie spotted black and yellow stripes. That was no sky raisin—it was one of those spicy sky snacks! He squinted suspiciously at the bee as she landed on a flower. He'd been there, done that, and wouldn't make that mistake again.

A sprinkler system gently sprayed the garden with a fine mist, and Billie danced through the water, twirling and jumping without a care. As the sprinklers turned off, he shook his body, and the water droplets flew off his feathers, which were becoming increasingly waterproof. "Look at me go!" he called out.

Wet dirt coated his beak as he dug into the moist soil and nibbled around.

"Got one!" he said as he swallowed a grub. He dug for juicy bugs and ate until his belly was plump and round. "Mmm, nature's candy. It doesn't get better than this!"

He followed a rocky path to a small pond, where three orange-and-white fish were swimming gracefully together. Billie stared in awe as the sunlight danced upon their scales like a scene from a dream. "Mind if I join you for a dip?" he asked, jumping in before they could answer. Paddling closer, he could see their beautifully flowing fins creating little ripples in the water.

He dunked his head under the water to get a closer look. The two larger fish were guarding the smaller one, as if to protect him from Billie's beak. "Oh." Billie's voice bubbled under the water as he realized that he might seem like a threat. "Don't mind me, I'm just passing through. And I already ate."

The three fish reminded him of his friendship with Marlie and Charlie. For a moment the sting of the memory hurt his heart. He knew that pretty soon his Fosterland friends would awaken and find that he had gone. But that was behind him now—so he hopped out of the pond and moved along, trying to leave the past in the past.

As he walked farther down the street, he came upon a curious obstacle.

Three tiny humans were sitting on the sidewalk, blocking the road ahead. Billie hid behind a streetlight and watched as they drew on the ground with colorful chalk, then hopped around as if to play some kind of jumping game. Not wanting to ruffle any feathers or get caught by the humans, Billie took a deep breath, then ran as fast as he could, hoping to go unnoticed.

It didn't work. A child noticed him instantly! The small human screamed in a language Billie didn't know, but he knew it could only mean one thing: he had to run.

He waddled through the hopscotch game as the children chased after him, squealing and shrieking with their arms outstretched. "Ahh!" he called out as he took a turn into a playground, where even more children chased after him, hooting and hollering. Darting around the schoolyard, he found himself jumping over jump ropes, running through a game of tag, and nearly getting flattened under a wooden seesaw. It was a wild-duck chase!

"Coming through!" he hollered as he exited the playground and made his way to a walking path in the park. Everywhere he looked, humans were pointing at him as if he didn't belong there. "Gotta go!" he screamed, waddling as fast as he could.

He rounded the corner and leaned against a fire hydrant. But his moment of relaxation was cut short by a barking dog who was making a beeline in his direction. "Ahh!" he screamed as the dog chomped at the air behind him. He ran as fast as he could to the edge of the park, where he sprinted through crunchy leaves and finally escaped into a patch of trees.

For a long time, Billie sat under the shade of a rock, catching his breath. The forest was quiet, and after the mayhem of the neighborhood park, he was grateful to be safe and alone. But as the sun began to set, his belly began to rumble, and he wondered where he would find dinner—or where he would sleep.

Suddenly, the crispy sound of foot-steps in the leaves got nearer, and Billie sat as still as a stone, closing his eyes and hoping it wasn't another pesky human trying to capture him, or that sneaky, snarling dog.

A gravelly voice approached, pass-ing by the rock. "So I tells her, I says: back up off my crab cakes, toots."

A second voice snickered, "Rufus, you crack me up!"

Billie's eyes widened at the name. He opened his eyes and quickly jumped out from behind the rock, shouting, "RUFUS?!"

Rufus shot into the air, his fur poofed out on all sides. "Ahhh!"

"Ahhh!" screamed Billie in automatic response.

As Rufus took in the sight of Billie, he wiped his fluffy brow and began to laugh. "Oh . . . my . . . gosh. You got me good, kid. You got me real good. Tough guy that I am, terrified by a little baby duck!"

"Bahaha! Did you see his face?" His friend fell to the forest floor, hysterical. "That was the funniest thing I've ever seen. Good for you, little one. You've got real spunk."

"He's a wild one," Rufus agreed.

Billie smiled from ear to ear.

"I'm Billie," he introduced himself.

"Pleased to make your acquaintance! I'm Pinkie," said Rufus's friend, smiling a huge, toothy grin. She was the strangest-looking feline Billie had ever seen, with a pointy snout, round ears, and a long, hairless tail. But she was so bubbly and friendly that Billie instantly warmed up to her.

"Billie, hey, good to meet ya," said Rufus, whose voice was powerful and low. "I'm . . . well, wait a minute. How did you already know my name?"

"Yeah," Pinkie added, "and what is a little yellow duck like you doing out in the forest at nighttime, anyway?"

Billie didn't even know where to start. "It's a really long story," he began, but he was interrupted by the sound of his own tummy rumbling. He looked down and frowned. "Sorry, I guess I haven't eaten in a while. . . ."

"Why don't you tell us your story over dinner?" Rufus offered, and began walking. "I know just the spot."

CHAPTER 9

The Primavera Heist

Billie waddled quickly to keep up with Rufus and Pinkie as they made their way through the moonlit forest. It was all so exhilarating!

"Almost there!" Pinkie said, looking back with a glimmer in her eye.

Up ahead, Billie could see strings of light glowing just beyond the trees and could hear the distant sound of people chattering and glasses clinking. They'd reached the edge of the woods, which backed up against a fine dining establishment.

"Bella Luna," Rufus whispered as they stood behind a tree, looking out at a patio. "It's one of our favorite Italian joints. A real classic."

Billie tilted his head. "You eat at restaurants?"

"Let's just say we get take-out." Rufus winked. "All right, Pinks, give 'em a good show."

Pinkie tiptoed to the edge of the restaurant, climbed to the roof, and scurried onto the striped awning over the patio. She wrapped her tail around a hanging lantern and shouted, "Ladies and gentlemen, for tonight's entertainment, I will be performing a dazzling acrobatic act for all you fine patrons!"

The restaurant-goers looked up at Pinkie on the lantern and gasped in unison. A startled man shot up in fright, accidentally flinging his salad across the patio. A woman grasped at her purse and backed up slowly, trembling. An entire screaming family ran into the parking lot. And a waiter carrying a huge platter of breadsticks dropped them onto the ground as he ran inside for help.

A breadstick three times the size of Billie rolled to his feet as he watched,

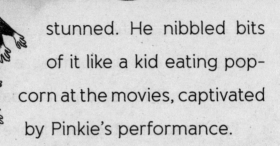

stunned. He nibbled bits of it like a kid eating popcorn at the movies, captivated by Pinkie's performance.

Pinkie laughed hysterically as she leapt from lantern to lantern, her impressive hairless tail grasping onto the metal as she dangled overhead. She had successfully startled away all the dinner guests.

Meanwhile, Rufus was running through the patio, seeing what the

restaurant had to offer. "Way to go, Pinks! Tonight we dine like royals!" he said as he leapt onto a table. "Ahaha!"

But before he could take even one nibble of a meatball, the waiter came back to shoo the mischievous pair away with a broom.

Rufus quickly grabbed a to-go bag someone left behind with his teeth and darted off toward the woods. Pinkie shoved a pawful of croutons into her front pocket and shouted, "Ya ain't

seen the last of us!" as she ran away, laughing.

Not wanting to be implicated in the crime or swept away with a broom, Billie quickly tore the biggest chunk of the bread that he could carry with him and darted away, too. The three giggled and yipped wildly as they sprinted through the leaves, and Billie felt alive and free.

Finally, they arrived outside a small shelter made of old wooden pallets in the middle of the woods. "Let's check the loot," Rufus said, licking his lips as he opened the to-go container to find a generous portion of salad, pasta with vegetables, and smoked salmon.

Billie chomped on chunks of romaine,

Pinkie slurped creamy noodles, and Rufus feasted on fish.

"I don't know why I assumed you two were hunters and gatherers," Billie said in between bites.

"Oh, we do plenty of that, too," Pinkie said, her mouth full of pasta.

"But even an ol' tom like me can't resist a fish fillet. I ain't gonna beg for it, though—I work hard and get it for myself!" Rufus said. "And my trusty associate here works hard for that pasta primavera, eh, Pinks?"

"What can I say? I like carbs!" She laughed, reaching into her pouch for a crunchy crouton. "Listen: opossums are called 'opportunistic scavengers.'

I see something I want, I take the opportunity."

Billie spit out his salad. "Opossum? I thought you were a cat!" he said.

"Funniest-lookin' cat I ever seen." Rufus chuckled. "Now, Billie. Tell us your story. How on earth did a little guy like you end up alone in the middle of the woods, and how exactly did you know my name?"

Billie sat up as tall as he could. "Well, it all started when . . ." He paused, not sure where to begin. It was such a long story! He scratched his head. "So, I'm a wild duck. Or at least . . . I thought I was a wild duck . . . but now I'm not so sure. For weeks, anyway, everyone has insisted that I'm not. I've been living in a place called Fosterland, where there are cats and ducks and humans—and they all think I'm meant to be someone's pet. . . ."

Pinkie and Rufus shot each other a knowing look.

Billie continued. "It was all so confusing until one day, I looked out the window, and I saw you, Rufus. Seeing you made me realize it's possible to choose which side of the door I want to live on. So I escaped through the mail slot, and now . . . ," he said, gently spreading his wings. "Here I am."

Rufus placed a paw on Billie's head and smiled. "I know exactly what you're going through. But let me tell you one thing: No one gets to tell you where you belong. Not me, not Pinks, not no one! And if you want to be part of this thing of ours, then, hey, welcome to the family. We'll call ourselves . . . *the Wild Childs*."

CHAPTER 10

The Wild Childs

Billie awoke to the refreshing feel-ing of morning dew beading up on his feathers as the sun began to rise. Over the past several weeks, his adult feathers had started to grow in, and now that he had longer, stron-ger plumage, he wasn't quite as fluffy as he used to be. He shook rapidly and dewdrops scattered off his waxy body, spritzing Rufus in the face.

Rufus was already awake and grooming himself. He paused with his tongue out and looked over at Billie. "Well, good morning to you, too."

"Eep! I didn't know you were already awake," Billie said. "You're an early riser!"

"Cats are crepuscular—we're most active at dusk and dawn," Rufus explained. "Opossums like Pinkie are nocturnal, so she'll probably be back from her nighttime shenanigans any minute. . . ."

Pinkie tumbled clumsily from a branch overhead. "Morning, fellas!" she said, rubbing her eyes. "No nighttime shenanigans for me. I was so full of pasta, I slept all night! Ha!"

"Well, what should we do today?" asked Billie.

"Whatever we want!" said Rufus. "That's the beauty of being a Wild Child. The world is your oyster."

"Mmm, oysters," Pinkie said.

The three decided to go on a hike to Pinkie's favorite spot. They stretched their limbs and headed up the mountain, one after another like three ducks in a row. As they walked, Rufus opened up about his history.

"I know just what you're goin' through, Bill. Believe it or not, I did some time on the inside myself. How do you think I got *this*?" he said, gesturing toward his ear tip—a sign that he had been neutered by a veterinarian. "Yeah, they'll poke ya and prod ya and try to turn ya into some kind of fancy house cat, but I hissed and muscled my way back outdoors. Good riddance."

Billie followed behind, kicking the dirt and hopping over rocks. "Only the cat decides!" he said, and Rufus and Pinkie cheered in agreement.

Pinkie paused at a fork in the trail and sniffed the ground with her pink nose. Her whiskers wiggled and she pointed to the path leading to the top of the mountain. "It's this way!" she said, and Billie followed.

"Yeah, I remember the old days," Rufus carried on, chewing a piece of grass as he hiked up the hill. "Back then, cats had to work for what they ate. Nowadays, these kittens have no respect for hard labor. They want everything served to them on a silver platter."

"With a little gravy on top!" Pinkie chortled.

"Things have changed, my friends. Things have changed. My nonno was the fiercest tom you ever saw. He would hack up a hairball if he saw his descendants sleeping on fluffy pillows and wearing little bells around their necks!" Rufus said, and spat out the chewed-up grass for dramatic effect.

"When I was on the inside, they tried to put me in a little hat," Billie said.

Pinkie guffawed. She picked up an acorn cap and stuck it on top of her head. "Oh, look at me, I'm domesticated! I wear a hat! I eat my food from a plastic baggie!"

Rufus picked up a pine cone and stuck it on his head, chuckling. "Look at me, I'm a pet! I poop in a sandbox! Bahaha!"

Billie laughed, too, but then felt a little guilty for making fun of his friends. It wasn't their fault they were pets, after all.

"You know, it isn't *that* bad in there,"

Billie admitted. "I did really like all my friends. Especially the other ducklings, Marlie and Charlie! A big part of me does miss them. It's just . . . I didn't feel like I could totally be my wildest self in Fosterland."

"Wildness comes from within, Billie. It ain't about where you are; it's about *who* you are," Rufus said. "Heck, I was the wildest I've ever been when I was in a cage, believe you me."

Pinkie paused, looking around. She hopped up onto a tree and climbed to the top to get a better view, then sniffed the air and squealed. "We're here!" she said, dropping down.

The three walked through a tall

patch of overgrown meadow grass and arrived at a lush patch of green foliage dotted with blue fruits. "Are these . . ." Billie asked, approaching a bush and sniffing cautiously, ". . . blueberries?"

"Ta-da!" Pinkie said, and started to

pluck them from the bushes and toss them into her mouth.

Billie couldn't believe it. He didn't know that blueberries could be wild— he thought they only came from the store! Maybe every animal and every fruit had a wild counterpart after all. He picked a ripe, juicy morsel from between the leaves and chomped down on the sweetest treat he had ever tasted. If only he could tell Marlie and Charlie that the bush berries were even more delicious than the ones that came from a plastic case. Maybe then they would understand him!

Pinkie and Billie snacked on sun-ripened berries under a thick canopy of green, while Rufus chased butterflies between the bushes. And as sugary as the fruits were, the whole experience felt a little bittersweet without Marlie and Charlie there by Billie's side, snacking away.

After they'd had their fill, the three lay in the center of the meadow and stared up at the clouds. They watched the airplanes flying up above and the hummingbirds that zipped around in search of wildflower nectar. Nature was all around them, and it seemed perfect.

"If this ain't livin'. . ." Rufus smiled. ". . . I don't know what is."

With the sun on his face and a berry-stained beak, Billie closed his eyes and felt content.

Suddenly, a shadow fell over them.

"Billie, duck!" Pinkie screamed.

"Yeah, I'm a duck, but you don't have to scream about—ahh!" Billie hollered, opening his eyes to the sudden sight of two hawks and their giant pointed talons zooming toward him. He ducked and rolled, running into the bushes.

Taking refuge underneath a fallen log, Rufus and Pinkie blocked the view of their small duckling friend and acted as lookouts.

"Nobody's hunting you on my watch," Rufus said, peeking out from the log cautiously. "Anyone who messes with you messes with us. That's what friends are for."

The hawks began to fly in a circle above them, their eyes darting around in search of their duckling prey.

Billie hid behind Rufus's and Pinkie's fluffy bodies and was grateful to have such protective pals. And their hiding trick had worked! After a few minutes, the hawks had given up and moved on.

"There we go, Billie: safe and sound. Looks like they've found someone else to hunt down the way," Pinkie said.

Billie stepped out from underneath the log and looked around, relieved.

From high up on the mountain, Billie could see everything: the Italian restaurant, the children's playground, the rose garden. And far in the distance, he could even see the home where Marlie and Charlie lived.

He looked to the sky and gulped. The hungry hawks were headed straight there—to his friends in Fosterland!

CHAPTER 11

Where's Billie?

The previous morning, Marlie and Charlie and the kittens had awoken to find that Billie wasn't in their bed.

They checked with Eloise, but she hadn't seen Billie either.

"Is he hiding somewhere?" Callooh cried. "Where could he have gone?"

All day, the kittens and the ducklings had searched the house for clues, looking behind pillows and in closets and under the couch. There was no trace of Billie anywhere, except one suspicious little feather in the mail slot. They'd tried to alert the human, but she just dropped their food off and left the house for hours and hours. They didn't even get to go outside for pool time!

As the day went on, they kept looking for some kind of sign of where Billie had gone. Marlie and Charlie dug through the garbage while the three little kittens rummaged through the human's bags.

"What's this?" Callay asked, pulling out a paper pamphlet from a purse. The pamphlet had three small Polaroid photos attached to it: one of Marlie, one of Charlie, and one of Billie. Inside the pages were photos of a serene sanctuary with green grass, fancy barns, and even a lake.

"Is this . . . our forever home?" Marlie cried. "It's beautiful. Oh, Charlie, can you imagine?"

"This place looks like Billie's dream home . . . ," Charlie said. "We can't go there without him. If we leave without him, he'll never find us again." Marlie wrapped her long neck around Charlie in a hug. The gesture was nice, but now that they were used to hugs including Billie, it felt like something was missing.

The sun was beginning to set, and

it was clear Billie wasn't coming home. Marlie, Charlie, and the kittens piled into bed together and cuddled for comfort.

"Maybe he's just in the back-yard," Mimsy tried to reassure Marlie and Charlie. "I'm sure he'll be there tomorrow. . . ."

"I hope you're right," Marlie said, sighing. "Maybe he'll be there at pool time, waiting for us."

"But what if he isn't?" Charlie asked her sister with tears in her eyes. "Then what will we do?"

"Well, we'll just have to call for him until he comes home . . . ," Marlie said. "He's out there somewhere, and he can't be that far. . . ."

The following day, they waited until it was time to swim, then ran frantically into the yard to look for Billie. The kittens watched from the screen door as Marlie waddled around the perimeter of the fence, and Charlie leapt into the pool, searching for their deep-sea-diving friend.

"He isn't here!" Charlie panicked.

"I don't see him either," cried Marlie. "We knew this was going to happen and we didn't listen! What if he's in danger? What if he got lost and wants to come home but can't find his way back to Fosterland?"

"We've got to do something!" Charlie agreed.

They talked with the kittens and all agreed that they needed to scream Billie's name as loud as they could, over and over, so that he might hear their cry and come home.

"*Billie! Billie! Billie!*" they screamed in unison. The kittens used their sharp claws to scale the side of the screen, clinging to it and hollering as loud as they could. Marlie and Charlie ran circles around the yard, shouting their friend's name, just hoping that it would somehow bring him home.

Billie couldn't hear them. They didn't know that he was far, far away on a mountaintop, too distant for a duckling to hear their cries.

But all their shouting and commotion did catch the attention of someone else: the two hungry hawks who were now headed straight for them.

"Those hawks are flying straight to Fosterland!" Billie screamed as he noticed where the birds of prey were heading. It was a beautiful day, and his friends would be paddling in the outside pool, not knowing what was coming for them. "Marlie and Charlie don't know how to defend themselves! Those are my friends. . . . I—I have to save them."

Pinkie and Rufus looked to the sky, then looked at Billie, who was already galloping down the mountain. They ran to catch up with him, and the three powered down the hillside, leaping over rocks and dashing through fields of flowers with lightning speed.

Zigzagging down the trails, Billie finally arrived at the bottom of the mountain, but when he looked to the sky, it was clear that the hawks had the advantage. They could fly straight to their target—and now they were almost to Fosterland.

"We have to run!" Billie screamed, scampering down the sidewalk in a frenzy. He darted through bike lanes, zipped past barking dogs on leashes, and scurried between the feet of passersby so quickly that his wild friends could hardly keep up.

"Billie! Hop on!" Pinkie screamed as they approached a skateboard in the center of the sidewalk. The three jumped onto the board and began ripping through the streets on four wheels, screaming at the top of their lungs.

"Lean right!" Pinkie called out, helping to narrowly avoid a collision with a fire hydrant. "Lean left!" she called, and the three wild skaters turned down the walking path that would lead to Fosterland.

Billie was in a panic. The hawks were circling faster and faster, and he knew he wouldn't make it to Fosterland in

time to save his friends, with or without wheels. He needed a more direct path. "There's got to be a faster way!" he cried.

Rufus placed a paw on Billie's back, his tabby coat blowing in the wind, and hollered, "Why don't you fly, Bill?"

Billie looked at Rufus, feeling completely powerless. "I told you! My wings don't work! Only wild ducks can fly!"

Rufus cleared his throat and hollered loud and clear, "Billie, I know you! You're as wild as they come! Fly, Billie. Fly!"

"Fly, Billie, fly!" Pinkie repeated. "Fly, Billie, fly!"

Billie dug down deep and thought

about Marlie and Charlie. He imagined them vulnerable in the pool, unaware of the danger that would soon be swooping down upon them. With a head start from the momentum of the skateboard, and a push from his friends, Billie opened his wings as wide as he could and flapped with a fierceness he'd never felt before.

Flap. Flap. Flap.

Suddenly . . . his feet lifted off the board.

And before he knew it, he was lifting higher . . . and higher . . . and higher . . . until the only thing beneath him was the summer breeze.

He was flying!

"He's doing it!" Pinkie cheered.

"That's our boy!" Rufus said, stopping the skateboard and watching from the ground as Billie the Wild Child ascended toward the sun, wild and free.

CHAPTER 12

Swoop

Soaring through the sky, Billie's heart raced with the thrill of his very first flight! He looked down at his wild friends disappearing into the distance, and his vision blurred as tears cascaded from his eyes, dropping over the city like a gentle rain.

He shook the tears from his face and looked ahead. There was no time to waste; he had a job to do! He pumped his wings, picking up speed as he flew straight toward the massive predatory birds.

As he zoomed closer to Fosterland, Billie could hear Marlie and Charlie in the yard, screaming his name. "Billie! Billie!"

"Look out!" he called down to them. He saw the joy on their faces when they spotted him, but that joy quickly turned to terror when they took in the two huge brown birds sharing the sky with Billie.

"Billie, look out!"

"Don't worry about me!" Billie yelled. "Hide, quick!"

"No, Billie, we're not leaving you!" Marlie and Charlie stayed in the grass, screaming for help from the guard, the kittens—from anyone!

Billie charged at the hunting birds as they began to swoop. "When you mess with my friends . . . you mess with . . ." He flew straight into the hawks, pushing them away fiercely with his final word: ". . . me!"

The hawks spun through the air and tumbled to the ground, completely disoriented.

Billie landed in the pool with an epic splash, and the two hawks scurried away, terrified of the tiny but mighty duckling who had thrown them off their hunt.

"And don't come back!" Billie huffed, flapping his wings in the water.

For a moment, Marlie, Charlie, and the kittens just stared at Billie.

Billie stepped out of the pool and shook the water off him. With his chest puffed out and his flight feathers at his side, Billie felt ten feet tall. He approached his friends, who were frozen, and said, "I had to come back. I couldn't let them hurt you."

Marlie and Charlie finally wrapped their wings around Billie in a huge group hug. Marlie stuttered as she finally spoke. "But . . . how . . . how? You . . . can fly? Are you really . . . a wild duck?"

Billie nodded. "I am. Or at least I think I am!"

"All this time you've been trying to tell us who you are . . . and we didn't believe you," Charlie said. "I'm so sorry."

"You saved our lives," Marlie said.

Billie closed his eyes and soaked in the incredible feeling of being seen— and celebrated—for who he really was.

Just then, Brillig shouted from the screen door, "That was legendary, dude!" and the others cheered in agreement.

For the rest of the day, the three ducks swam in the pool, ate sky raisins, and caught up on Billie's wild adventures. Billie told them all about Rufus and Pinkie and the great pasta con and how they'd even hiked to the top of a mountain together.

"Wait a minute. You mean to tell me blueberries *grow on trees*?" Charlie asked.

"Not exactly," Billie said. "More like big bushes—and as far as the eye can see! They were so delicious, but all I could think about the entire time was how it would have been better if you two were there to enjoy them with me." He dove under the water and swam in circles under Marlie's and Charlie's feet, just like he used to do.

When he popped up, Marlie and Charlie giggled with merriment. They were so happy to be reunited with their quirky, silly, uniquely wild friend Billie.

"There's something we have to talk to you about, Billie," Marlie said. "I think . . . our time in Fosterland is almost over."

"We know you probably want to

get back out there to the mountain . . . but if you'll just hear us out for two minutes . . . we learned something that we think could convince you to join us—" Charlie started but was quickly interrupted by an eager Billie.

"Say no more," Billie said. "I've made up my mind: I'm staying with the two of you. I learned that I have a wild heart no matter where I am . . . and that no matter where I go, I want to be with my two best friends."

"You mean it?" Marlie asked.

"I mean it," Billie said, assuredly.

Marlie and Charlie flapped their wings with joy. They began to sing, "Birds of a feather . . . We stick together. . . ."

Billie chimed in, until all three of them were singing at the top of their lungs: "Birds of a feather—best friends forever!"

CHAPTER 13

The Best of Both Worlds

The day had come for everyone to graduate from foster care and head to their forever homes. Billie, Marlie, and Charlie lined up at the door and said goodbye to the kittens, who were preparing for their big adoption day.

"I truly wish you the best," Billie said as he hugged the kittens. "You guys are going to be awesome lap cats, so loved and spoiled. And, hey—don't forget your paper hats," he added, winking.

The three ducklings hopped into a big metal crate in the backseat of a truck and waved goodbye to Foster-land. With every bump in the road, Billie thought about the hurdles he'd already overcome in life: the cardboard box that had separated him from his birthplace, all the people and animals that had misunderstood him, and the friends who had helped him to heal. He took a deep breath and reminded himself that no matter where he ended up, he would belong—because he knew who he was, and he would carry that with him always.

The truck pulled off on a dirt road, and Billie gulped. It was the moment of truth.

As the truck door opened, the scent of wildflowers filled the air. Billie could hear the sounds of birds chirping and donkeys braying. Long-necked llamas chewed grass with their alpaca friends, and chickens scratched the ground for seeds. In the distance, a family of wild deer walked through the woods together.

Billie hopped out of the crate and onto the grass and looked around excitedly.

"Welcome to your forever home, friends!" said a little pink pig named

Ella with a small songbird resting on her head. "We are a sanctuary for all animals—a place where you can be anyone you want to be."

Marlie and Charlie stepped out of the truck and looked around, oohing and aahing. It was the place they had seen pictured in the pamphlet—but in real life it was even better!

"Whoa! This place is bigger than it looked in the photographs!" Marlie said.

"Photographs?" Billie asked but was immediately distracted by a sky raisin flying by.

"We're here! We're really here! Ain't it just a dream?" Charlie cheered.

Marlie and Charlie started spinning in circles, cheering and singing and bumping their butts. "So much to see! So much to eat! So much to do!"

Marlie paused. "And, Billie . . . you don't even know the best part—do you?"

Billie turned around, already nibbling on a fly. "The best part?" he said with his mouth full.

Marlie and Charlie jumped up and down. "Follow us!"

Marlie's feet waddled rapidly underneath her. Charlie followed close behind. And Billie, the smallest but fiercest, was third in the row, not knowing the secret that his friends had seen in the pamphlet days before.

"It's got to be here somewhere!" Marlie said as they ran faster and faster.

"Up ahead!" Charlie squealed.

The three ran with wild abandon until suddenly Billie saw it: the glassy, shimmering surface of a serene body of water.

". . . *It's a lake!*" Billie screamed, flapping with such fervor that he lifted from the ground and flew straight ahead. With his wings spread wide and his webbed feet outstretched, he landed in the water with a joyful splash, creating ripples on the surface that seemed to surround him with dancing sunlight. *"A real lake!"*

Marlie and Charlie waddled behind, cheering for their friend's impressive flight and leaping in the water to join him in a swim.

From that day on, Billie, Marlie, and Charlie spent their days in a nurturing sanctuary that offered them the best of both worlds. They had the safety of a barn to sleep in and a daily menu of garden-fresh vegetables and fruits— but they also had the freedom of an expansive territory where they could explore nature.

Domesticated or wild, all were welcome there and lived together in harmony. Friendly goats ate grass while opossums watched from the trees above. Domestic turkeys shared strawberries with wild turkeys passing through. Feral felines lay in sunbeams as pet cats watched from the farmhouse window, purring in their cat trees. And plenty of wild birds, like blue herons and egrets, visited at the edge of the lake where Billie and his duck friends swam each day.

Marlie and Charlie grew into beautiful, large white ducks, and while they never could fly, they did love to swim. Billie became a white duck, too—but small and nimble and with the same wild spirit he'd always had as a boy.

"Billie the Wild Child," he called him-

self, though he still didn't fully understand the nature of his wildness—until
one day he finally got his answer.

The three white ducks were swimming in the lake when suddenly two
brown ducks flew in. Swimming
nearer, one of them looked at Billie
and gasped.

"Why, it's a white mallard!" the wild
duck said. "You're one of us—but in
such a rare color!"

"I've only heard stories of unicorns
like you," the other agreed. "You really
are special, you know that?"

Billie smiled. He dove under the
water, deep-sea diving beneath the
paddling feet of Marlie, Charlie, and his

new wild friends, and felt great pride in who he was.

He popped to the surface of the lake and let out a happy, raspy quack.

He was exactly where he belonged.

The True Story
of Billie

When Billie was just a day or two old, he was brought to a wildlife center in San Diego, California, along with several brown-and-yellow ducklings. Because he was solid yellow, he was assumed to be a domestic breed of duckling and was placed in the animal shelter instead of with the other wild ducklings. That's how I ended up picking up Billie as a foster baby!

Knowing that ducklings are happiest in a group, I didn't want him to be alone. I asked around to see if there were any other ducklings in need, and fortunately a local veterinarian knew of two ducklings who needed to be rescued, too. We named them Marlie and Charlie, and Billie loved them right away, even though he was so tiny by comparison. The three of them became instant best friends and stuck together always.

Billie, Marlie, and Charlie loved to swim in an outdoor dog pool every day, where we would give them bits of shredded romaine lettuce and special snacks like berries. Billie was an expert swimmer who could hold his breath for long periods of time, and he would glide around the bottom of the pool gleefully while the girls would float on the surface. Sometimes we would get in the pool with them, too! After they swam, they'd dig in the grass for bugs and preen in the sunshine.

From the beginning, it was obvious that Billie was different from his new duckling friends. Not only was he much smaller, but he was much feistier, too! While Marlie and Charlie loved to be petted and held, Billie was a little rebel who never quite warmed up to humans (unless they had blueberries or cherry tomatoes . . . then he'd make an exception). We always wondered if there had been a mix-up at the wildlife center and if he was, in fact, a wild duckling, but there was no way to know for sure until he was grown.

Billie and his friends were eventually adopted by Morningside Farm Sanctuary, a wonderful all-species animal haven outside of Eugene, Oregon. As he grew into an adult, it became clear that he was actually a white mallard—a special coloration of a wild duck breed! He is still much smaller than the girls and is the only one of the three who can fly. Billie gave everyone a big scare when he first got his flight feathers and took off for a neighboring field, but after his momentary adventure, he came right back and never left again!

Now life at the sanctuary is paradise for Billie. Some of his favorite activities include eating the wild berries that grow outside, hanging out in his A-frame duck house, and swimming all day with his two best friends, Marlie and Charlie.

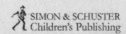